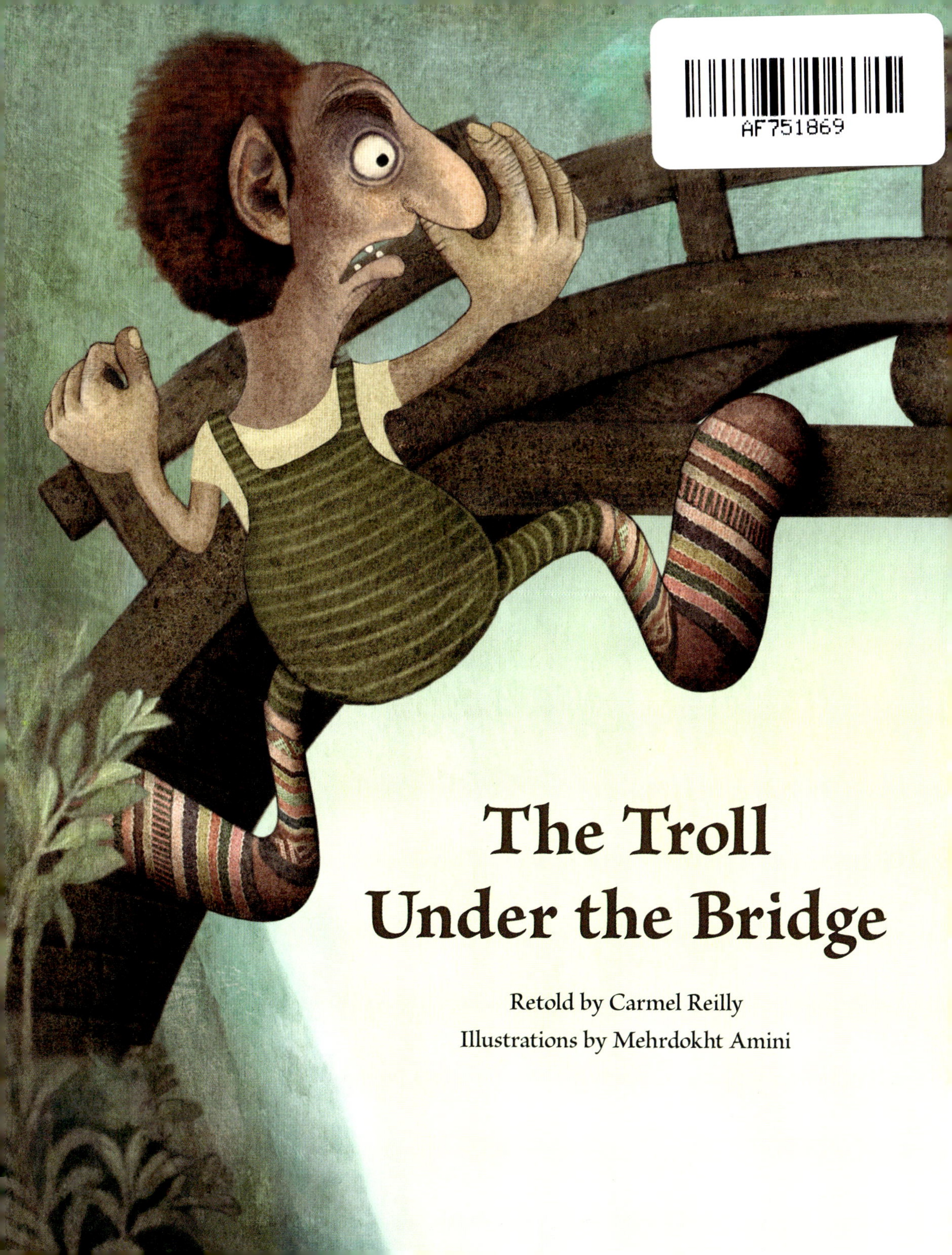

The Troll Under the Bridge

Retold by Carmel Reilly

Illustrations by Mehrdokht Amini

Once upon a time,
there was a mean old troll
who lived under a bridge.

One day,
he was feeling very hungry.

"What can I eat?" he said.

Just then,
something walked
over the bridge above him.

The troll looked over the top
of the bridge
and saw a small goat.

The troll jumped onto the bridge.

"Who are you?" he roared.
"And what do you want?"

"I'm Little Billy Goat Gruff,"
said the goat.
"I want to go across the bridge."

"You are not going to do that,"
roared the troll.
"Because I'm going to gobble you up!"

"I'm too small to eat!"
cried Little Billy Goat Gruff.

"But my brother is coming soon.
He's much bigger than I am
and much better to eat."

“Is he?” said the troll.
“All right. Off you go, then.”

The little goat
ran over the bridge.

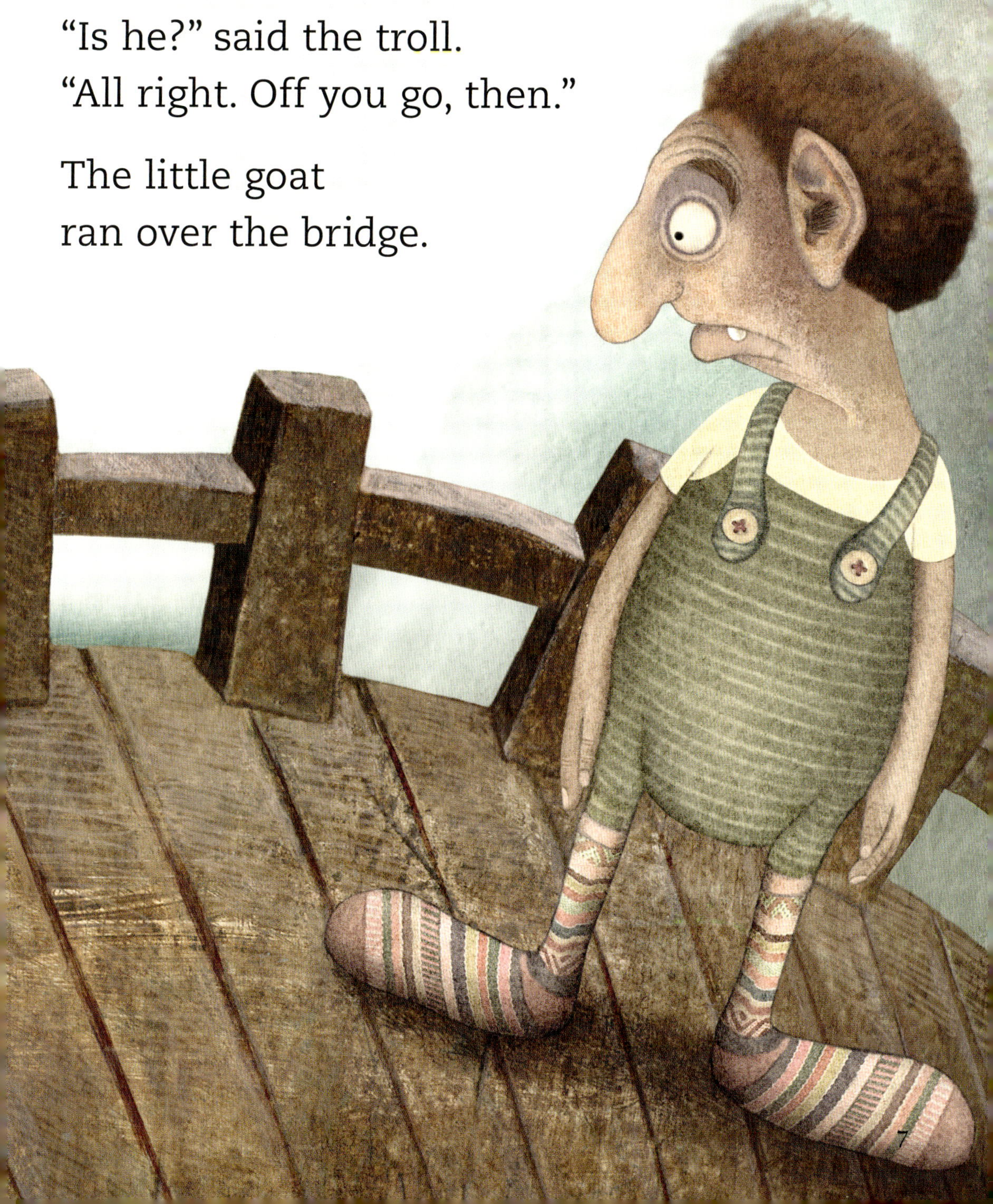

The troll waited
under the bridge
until the next goat
came along.

The troll jumped up.

"Who are you?" he roared.
"And what do you want?"

"I'm Middle-sized Billy Goat Gruff.
I want to go across the bridge,"
he said.

"Well, I'm going to gobble you up!"
roared the troll.

"No!" cried the middle-sized goat.
"My big brother is coming soon.
He will be much better
to eat than me."

"Will he?" said the troll.
"All right. Off you go."

The middle-sized goat
ran over the bridge.

When the next goat
came to the bridge,
the troll got a big surprise.
This billy goat was enormous.

"I'm Great Big Billy Goat Gruff,"
he said.
"And you are not going
to gobble me up."

The big goat pushed the troll
off the bridge
and into the water.

The troll floated along the river.

By the time he got out
of the water,
he was **very** hungry.

Then he saw a vegetable garden
and some fruit trees.
He ran over and started eating.

He gobbled up carrots and peas
and apples.

"No one told me that fruit and vegetables were so good!" said the troll.

From that day on,
the troll ate lots of fruit and vegetables.

And he never tried to eat billy goats again.